3/07

ALLEN COUNTY PUBLIC LIBRARY

3 1833 05176 6860

HOLIDAY COLLECTION

P9-DGY-736

Christmas Turtles

For My Grandmother, Annie May Lund Francis, and my boys, Samuel and Gideon.

Special thanks to my husband, Boyd Denson, and my parents,
Richard and Pam Clayton, for all your loving support (and
babysitting) and to my professor, Dr. Mary Brown, for cracking me
open and adding caramel and chocolate.

~ Sara Ann

Text Copyright © 2006 Sara Ann Denson
Illustrations Copyright © 2006 Tara McMillen

Title: Christmas Turtles
Author: Sara Ann Denson
Illustrator: Tara McMillen

ISBN: 0-9769017-6-5
ISBN-13: 978-0-9769017-6-1
LCCN: 2006904387
SAN: 256-5994

Library of Congress Cataloging-in-Publication Data:
Christmas Turtles/written by Sara Ann Denson
Summary: Christmas story about a grandmother's holiday tradition of
making chocolate turtles with her grandchildren.

1. Grandparent and Child - Juvenile Fiction.
2 Christmas - Juvenile Fiction

I. Denson, Sara Ann
II. Title

PURPLE SKY PUBLISHING
PO Box 12013, Parkville, MO 64152
www.purpleskypublishing.com

Design & Layout: Phat Vuong

Printed in China

Christmas Turtles

Written by Sara Ann Denson

Illustrated by Tara McMillen

Between a little gray house and two gray barns grew four leafy green pecan trees. Grandma planted a tree when each of her four grandchildren were born: one for Talia, one for Jeanna, one for Matthew, and one for me. They grew tall and spindly as our legs shot up and our hair grew out and our smiles became toothy, then toothless, and toothy again.

Every fall, when the yellow and orange leaves blew from the trees and circled through the air, the pecans ripened and fell to the ground. Each afternoon, as Grandma walked to the barn to feed the animals, she could hear the sound of the pecans as they hit the tin barn roof: ping, ping, ping. On her way back to the house, she bent close to the ground searching the bright colored leaves for the small brown nuts. Grandma gathered them into the folds of her skirt and carried them to the wooden crate on the front porch.

When most of the leaves had fallen and the days turned gray and chilly, the moms and dads and aunts and uncles gathered at Grandma's house to help Grandpa plant the winter wheat. The cousins gathered on the old stone porch. We sat and watched as the tractor moved back and forth across the fields until it became a speck on the horizon, barely visible against the setting sun. That was when Grandma brought out the magic Christmas tin. It was dented and worn, but the faded burgundies and blues still formed tiny pictures of Snowmen and Reindeer.

"Come bring the pecans," Grandma announced, handing the tin to Talia. Jeanna, Matthew and I pushed the heavy crate full of pecans toward Grandma. Grandma rocked back and forth in her white rocking chair and cracked the first pecan: crack, crack, crack. She turned it around in her knobby hands until the shell was criss-crossed and soft. Then she handed the cracked pecan to me and wiggled her weathered fingers.

"Why do you do that?" I asked, wiggling my fingers just like her.

"Because squeezing makes my hands hurt," she said. "Here. You try, Sara Ann." She handed me the silver nutcracker. I squeezed and squeezed and squeezed until the shell broke, and I squished the nut inside. "Now you try," she told Jeanna, and Jeanna cracked it once and pinched her thumb. "Don't worry," said Grandma. "Your hands will get stronger." Then, Jeanna and I peeled off the bits of shell from the pecans Grandma cracked until we could see two perfect, golden halves. Talia, because she was the oldest, stacked the pecan halves in the tin until it was half-full. Matthew, because he was the youngest, carried the tin to the freezer.

"Will they come again this year?" we asked as Grandma shut the freezer door. Grandma only smiled.

Each Christmas season, all the moms and dads and aunts and uncles returned to Grandma's farm. The cousins, Talia, Jeanna, Matthew and I, ran to look in the freezer. We pulled out the frosty tin and popped off the lid. The cold air swirled around us as we saw that the pecans had been magically transformed. They emerged with tan, caramel bodies and black, chocolate shells; all delicately wrapped in pink plastic. The pecans stuck out like turtle feet. "Chocolate covered turtles!" we squealed in delight as we peeled back the wrappers. We crunched through the frozen shells just as the rest of the family came running to eat the turtles.

We scurried away, to all
our secret places, hiding the
turtles from the adults. We put
them inside the old purses in
the toy box. We reached up into
the bottom of Grandma's sewing
machine and behind the old, upright
piano with two stiff keys. We giggled
behind the bedroom door as one turtle
after another melted softly in our mouths.

My mom put her arms around me and
tickled me until I gave her a bite. "But
where do they come from?" I asked her,
as chocolate dribbled down our chins.
"Do the elves really make them?"

"No," Mom told me.
"It's someone who loves you even
more than the elves."

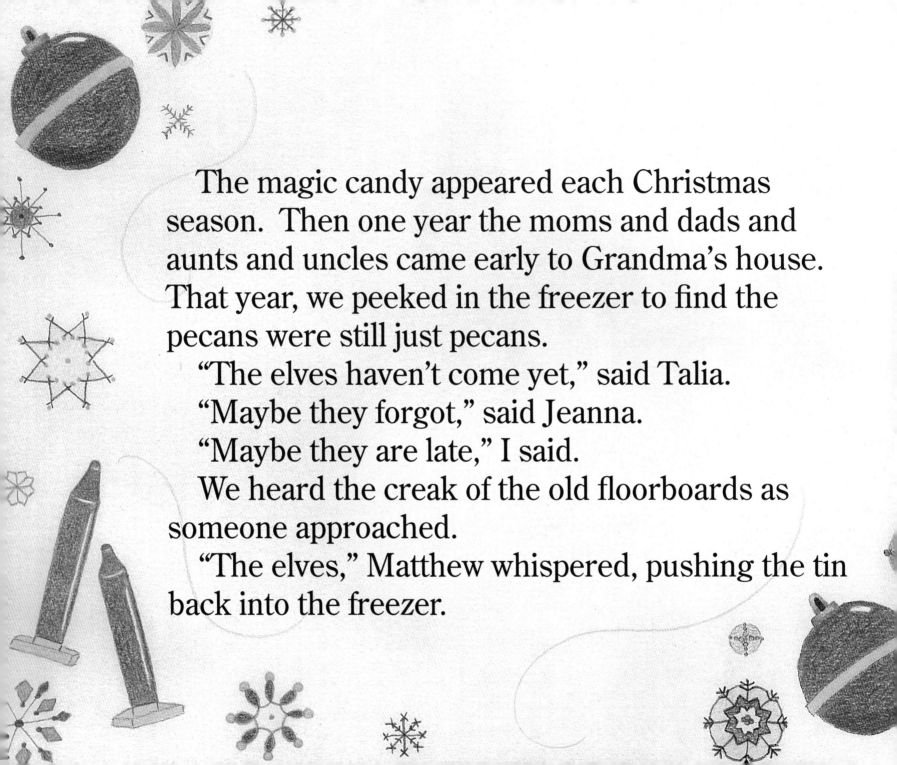

The magic candy appeared each Christmas season. Then one year the moms and dads and aunts and uncles came early to Grandma's house. That year, we peeked in the freezer to find the pecans were still just pecans.

"The elves haven't come yet," said Talia.

"Maybe they forgot," said Jeanna.

"Maybe they are late," I said.

We heard the creak of the old floorboards as someone approached.

"The elves," Matthew whispered, pushing the tin back into the freezer.

We darted under the kitchen table and peeked from under the vinyl tablecloth. It was Grandma! She opened the freezer and the cold, frosty air swirled around her as she pulled out the magical tin. Then, she laid the pecans in rows of two across shimmering aluminum foil spread over the countertop.

"Come out from there, you four," Grandma called to us as she poured brown sugar and cream into her red pot.

We inched from under the table to get a closer look. Grandma stirred the brown liquid until it bubbled. It bubbled higher and higher until it was light cream and threatened to tumble over the edge of the pot like popcorn. Grandma stirred faster. We stood at the stove until our backs hurt and the heels of our feet throbbed. Stirring on, Grandma only shifted her weight and stretched her hunched back. The red line on her candy thermometer slowly moved upward until the soft tan liquid thickened and turned dark amber. Grandma pulled the pan from the burner.

Next, Grandma dripped the hot caramel onto the pecans to form a glistening turtle body. We smiled and licked our lips. "Don't touch," Grandma warned softly. "Not until it cools." She moved faster so that each set of pecans received a caramel body before the candy thickened.

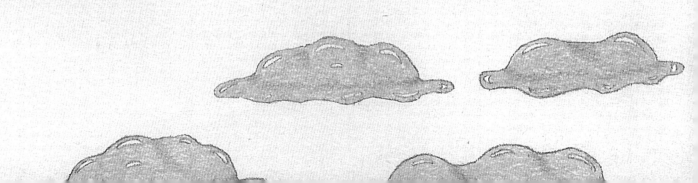

Then, Grandma put another red pan on the stove. She poured in the chocolate chips and added a cap full of oil. "Would you like to stir?" she asked us, letting me climb onto a chair. I leaned over the pan and felt the heat against my face. I pushed my spoon through the thick chocolate until it was Talia's turn to try.

When the chocolate melted into a shiny pool, Grandma poured it over each piece of candy. She gave each of us a spoon and we smoothed the chocolate across the turtle bodies.

"Can we eat them? Can we eat them?" we pleaded when we finished and began to lick the spoons.

"Not until the chocolate hardens," Grandma said. So we waited, watching what seemed like miles of holiday candy.

"Not until the chocolate hardens," she told me as I pushed my finger into one of the soft shells an hour later.

"Not until the chocolate hardens," she warned near suppertime as Jeanna picked one up and smelled the rich, sweet scent.

Finally, Grandma said, "They're ready."

We rushed to the kitchen with moms and dads and aunts and uncles at our heels. All of us tilted our heads back to let the first Christmas turtle drop into our watering mouths — except for Grandma.

Grandma smiled as she watched us eat. She didn't take a turtle for herself. "Won't you eat one, Grandma?" I asked, tasting the caramel filling my cheeks.

Grandma shook her head. "I can't eat them," she said. "I just make them to see the glow in your eyes."

My eyes widened as I plucked another turtle from the aluminum foil. "You can't?" I asked, and suddenly I knew. I knew just how much Grandma loved us all. She loved Talia enough to stoop across the yard gathering pecans. She loved Jeanna enough to crack shells when it hurt her hands. She loved Matthew enough to hunch over a hot stove as her back ached and her feet throbbed. She loved me enough to make turtles every year so we could scamper like squirrels hiding our treasure around her house. I threw my arms around Grandma. "I love you, too, Grandma," I whispered.

Christmas Turtles

Ingredients:

1	cup butter
1	16 oz package of brown sugar (2 cups)
1	16 oz carton of heavy whipping cream (2 cups)
1	cup light corn syrup
1	24 oz bag of chocolate chips
1	16 oz bag of pecan halves

Also needed:
  aluminum foil or wax paper
  6 quart saucepan
  large spoon
  candy thermometer
  plastic wrap

- Feet — Lay out all of the pecan halves in groups of two, two inches apart, on several sheets of buttered aluminum foil or wax paper.
- Body — Mix the butter, brown sugar, whipping cream, and corn syrup in a 6 quart saucepan. Using a large spoon, stir constantly over medium-high heat, letting the mixture boil. Clip a candy thermometer onto the edge and continue stirring until the thermometer reads 245–248 degrees. Remove saucepan from heat and immediately begin spooning small globs of caramel onto the pecan halves to cover the feet before the caramel hardens.
- Shell — Melt 24oz package of chocolate chips according to package instructions. Spoon melted chocolate over the bodies, smearing thickly to coat.
- Packaging — Wrap the turtles in individual squares of plastic wrap to keep them from sticking together. Place the turtles in a magic Christmas tin.